Hello Wildcat!

Aimee Aryal

Illustrated by Blair Cooper

MASCOT BOOKS™

www.mascotbooks.com

It was a beautiful day at the
University of Kentucky.

The Wildcat was on his way to
Rupp Arena to watch a basketball game.

He walked across the Great Lawn
and past the Main Building.

A professor passing by said,
"Hello Wildcat!"

The Wildcat stopped in front of
the Student Center.

Two students on their way to class
waved, "Hello Wildcat!"

The Wildcat walked to
William T. Young Library.

A librarian who works inside
said, "Hello Wildcat!"

The Wildcat went over to
Commonwealth Stadium where the
Wildcats play football.

A group of Kentucky fans standing nearby shouted, "Hello Wildcat!"

It was almost time for the basketball game. As the Wildcat walked to Rupp Arena, he passed by some alumni.

The alumni remembered the Wildcat
from when they went to UK.
They said, "Hello, again, Wildcat!"

Finally, the Wildcat
arrived at the game.

As he ran onto the basketball court,
the crowd cheered, "Go Big Blue!"

The Wildcat watched the game from the sidelines and cheered for the team.

The Wildcats scored a basket!
The players shouted,
"Slam Dunk Wildcat!"

At half-time, the Wildcat and Scratch
listened to the Pep Band play.

The crowd sang,
"On! On! U of K."

The Kentucky Wildcats
won the game!

The Wildcat gave Coach Smith
a high-five. The coach said,
"Great game Wildcat!"

After the basketball game,
the Wildcat was tired. It had been a
long day at the University of Kentucky.

He walked home and climbed into bed.

"Goodnight Wildcat."

For Anna and Maya,
and all of the Wildcat's little fans. ~ AA

To Peter, Anya, and Merril. These books
would not have been possible without you. ~ BC

Special thanks to:

Jason Schlafer

Tubby Smith

For information please contact Mascot Books,
P.O. Box 220157, Chantilly, VA 20153-0157.

UNIVERSITY OF KENTUCKY, UK, KENTUCKY, WILDCATS, KENTUCKY WILDCATS
and GO BIG BLUE are trademarks or registered trademarks of the University of Kentucky
and are used under license.

ISBN: 1-932888-33-0

Printed in the United States.

www.mascotbooks.com